This Walker book belongs to:

_____

_____

_____

For Emile, Elsie
and Emma ~ M.R.

For the lost and found
of Dalston ~ J.S.

First published 2009 by Walker Books Ltd
87 Vauxhall Walk, London SE11 5HJ

This edition published 2010

10 9 8 7 6 5 4 3 2 1

Text © 2009 Michael Rosen
Illustrations © 2009 Joel Stewart

The right of Michael Rosen and Joel Stewart to be identified as author and illustrator respectively of this work
has been asserted by them in accordance with the Copyright, Designs and Patents Act 1988

This book has been typeset in Opti Typo Roman and Regular Joe

Printed in China

British Library Cataloguing in Publication Data:
a catalogue record for this book is available from the British Library

ISBN 978-1-4063-2655-0

www.walker.co.uk

RED TED
AND THE
LOST
THINGS

MICHAEL ROSEN
JOEL STEWART

WALKER BOOKS
AND SUBSIDIARIES
LONDON · BOSTON · SYDNEY · AUCKLAND

One day a little bear called Red Ted was left on a train. He found himself being put on a shelf by a Man in a Hat...

Up you go!

4

And Red Ted burst into tears.

Next morning,
when the
Man in the Hat
came in,
Red Ted hopped
down off the shelf.

13

So Crocodile hopped down off the shelf too, and together they rushed out of the door.

And they followed the signs.

Outside, Red Ted stopped.
So Crocodile stopped.

We're still lost, aren't we? I knew things would go wrong.

It won't stay like this. Something will happen.

16

And just then a voice said:

It was a cat.

And the cat turned to go.

But then she stopped and sniffed.

Do I smell cheese? Mmmmmmmmm, lovely!

I think I know where your home is. Follow me.

So they followed the cat, and as they walked along she sang a little song:

I'm a cat
And I do
as I please,
I'm a cat
And I love
cheese!

After a while it began to rain.

And they did.

When the rain stopped,
they walked on.
Under a bridge.
Through the market.
Down an alley.

So Crocodile showed
the great big dog his
great big teeth.

The great big dog didn't like Crocodile's great big teeth and it ran away.

They walked on and came round a corner.

Red Ted stopped.

You're lost again, aren't you? You don't know where we are.

I do! I do!

All three of them rushed up to the front door.

But there was nobody home.

She's not here. No one's here. She's gone away for ever! And now I'll never see Stevie ever again!

Now I won't get any cheese.

I knew it was too good to be true.

Things were looking bad.

Then, suddenly, round the corner, came ... Stevie!

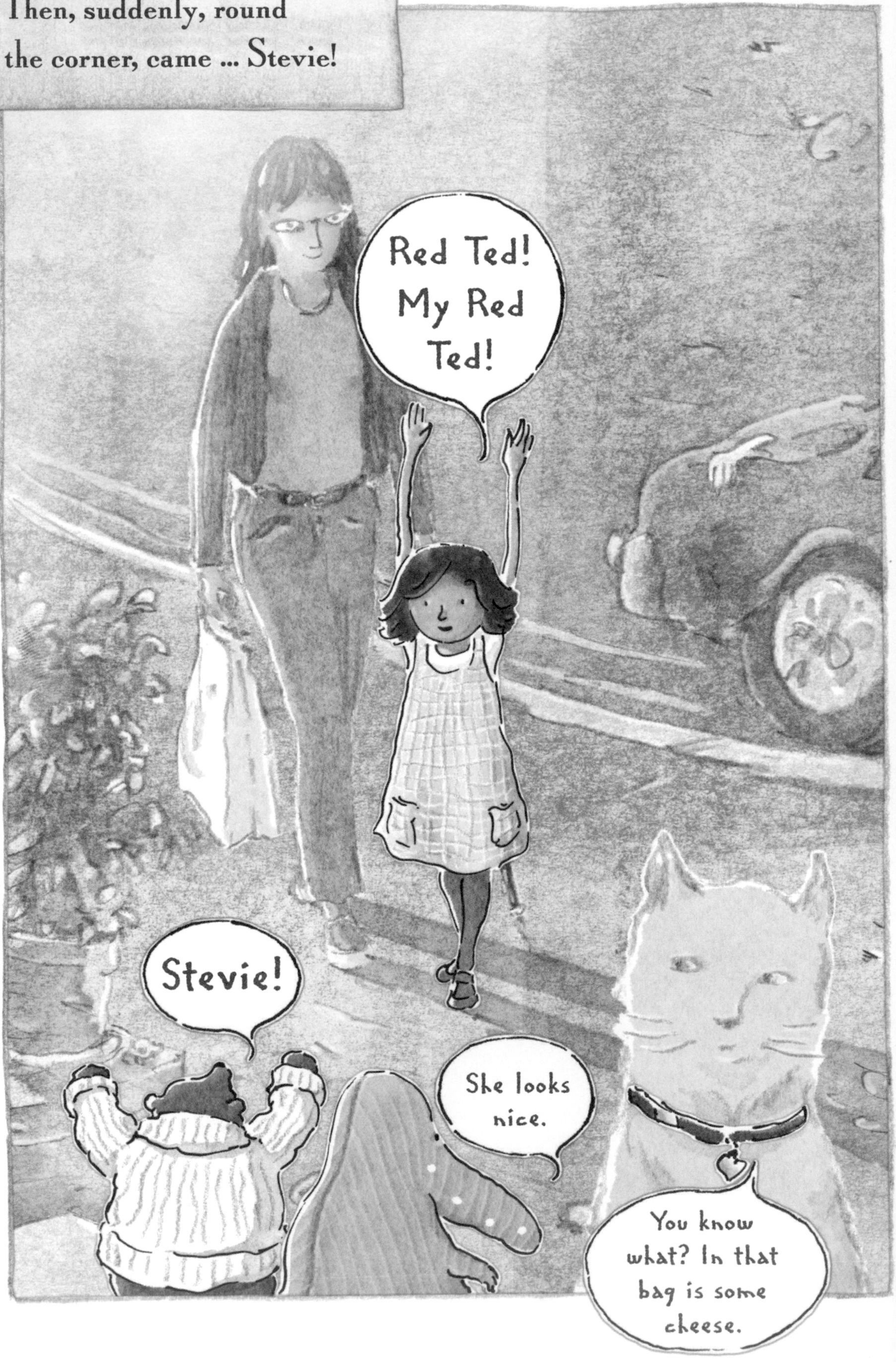

That night when she went
to bed, Stevie was happy.
Crocodile was happy.
The cat was happy.
But no one was happier
than Red Ted, who'd found
Stevie again and who wasn't
lost any more.